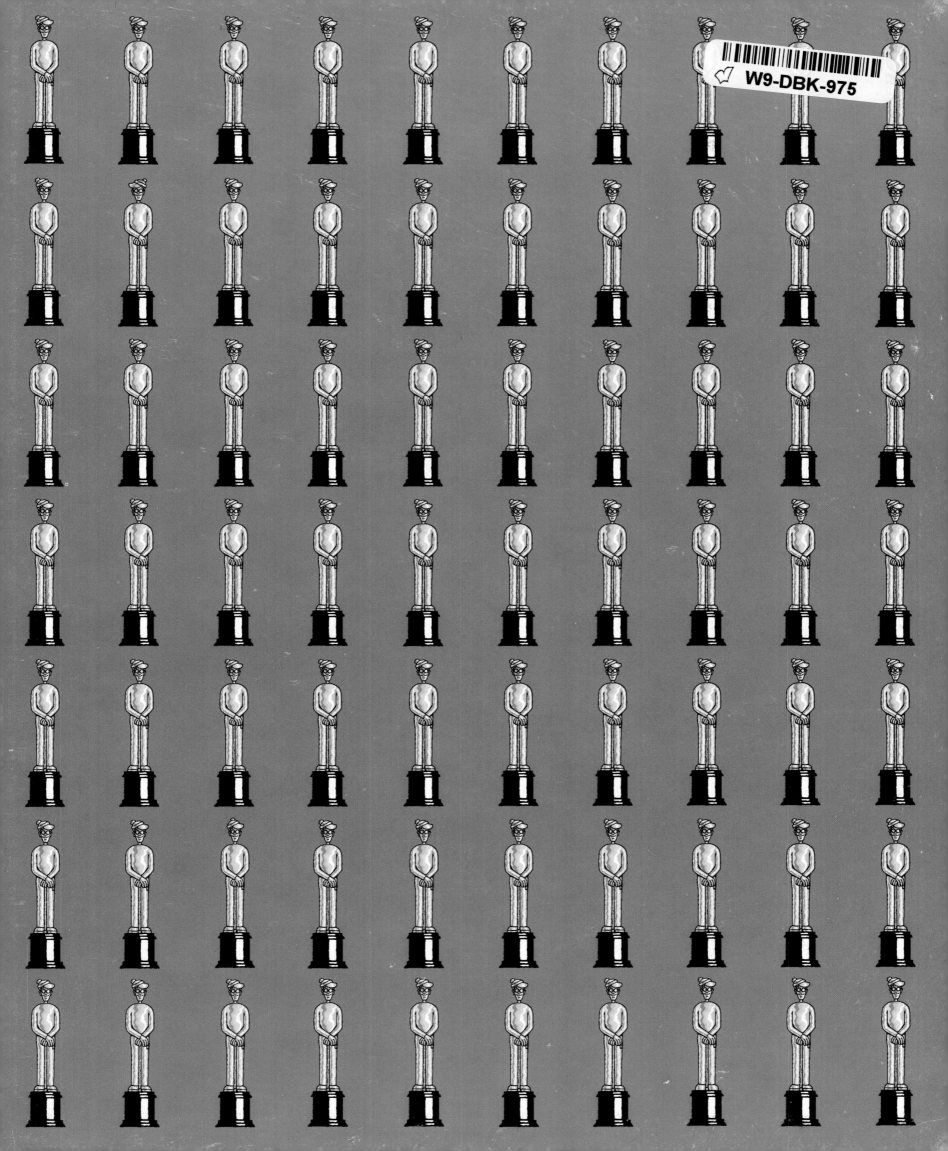

TO ELIZABETH, MIKE, STEVE, EDDY, AND TERRY

FOR ALL THEIR HELP AND ENCOURAGEMENT

First U.S. edition 1993
Published in Great Britain in 1993 by Walker Books Ltd., London.
Library of Congress Cataloging-in-Publication Data is available.
Library of Congress Catalog Card Number 91-71819

ISBN 1-56402-044-4 (trade)
ISBN 1-56402-294-3 (lib. bdg.)

10 9 8 7 6 5 4 3 2 1

Color separations by Lamplight Colour Ltd., London, and Dot Gradations Ltd., Essex
Printed in Italy by Printers SRL, Trento. Bound in Italy by L.E.G.O., Vicenza

Candlewick Press
2067 Massachusetts Avenue
Cambridge, Massachusetts 02140

WHERE'S WALDO? IN HOLLYWOOD

MARTIN HANDFORD

CANDLEWICK PRESS
CAMBRIDGE, MASSACHUSETTS

A DREAM COME TRUE

WOW, WALDO-WATCHERS, THIS IS FANTASTIC. I'M REALLY IN HOLLYWOOD! LOOK AT THE FILM PEOPLE EVERYWHERE – I WONDER WHAT MOVIES THEY'RE MAKING. THIS IS MY DREAM COME TRUE ... TO MEET THE DIRECTORS AND ACTORS, TO WALK THROUGH THE CROWDS OF EXTRAS, TO SEE BEHIND THE SCENES! PHEW, I WONDER IF I'LL APPEAR IN A MOVIE MYSELF!

★ ★ ★ WHAT TO LOOK FOR IN HOLLYWOOD! ★ ★ ★

WELCOME TO TINSELTOWN, WALDO-WATCHERS! THESE ARE THE PEOPLE AND THINGS TO LOOK FOR AS YOU WALK THROUGH THE MOVIE SETS WITH WALDO:

★ FIRST (OF COURSE!) WHERE'S WALDO?

★ NEXT FIND WALDO'S CANINE COMPANION, WOOF – REMEMBER, ALL YOU CAN SEE IS HIS TAIL!

★ THEN FIND WALDO'S FRIEND, WENDA!

★ ABRACADABRA! HOCUS POCUS! NOW FOCUS IN ON THE GREAT MAGICIAN, WIZARD WHITEBEARD!

★ BOO! HISS! LAST COMES THE BAD GUY, ODLAW – HE'S WICKED ENOUGH TO STEAL THE SCENE!

★ KEEP ON SEARCHING! THERE'S MORE TO FIND! ★

★ ON EVERY SET FIND WALDO'S LOST KEY!

★ ON EVERY SET FIND WOOF'S LOST BONE!

★ ON EVERY SET FIND WIZARD WHITEBEARD'S SCROLL!

★ ON EVERY SET MAKE YOURSELF REALLY USEFUL – FIND A MISSING CAN OF FILM!

★ ★ ★ ★ ★ ★ AND MORE AND MORE! ★ ★ ★ ★ ★ ★

EACH OF THE FOUR POSTERS ON THE WALL OVER THERE IS PART OF ONE OF THE MOVIE SETS WALDO IS ABOUT TO VISIT.

★ FIND OUT WHERE THE POSTERS COME FROM.

★ THEN SPOT ANY DIFFERENCES BETWEEN THE POSTERS AND THE SETS.

SHHH! THIS IS A SILENT MOVIE

SO THIS IS HOW THE HOLLYWOOD DREAM BEGAN — WITH SILENT MOVIES MADE IN BLACK AND WHITE. IT LOOKS CRAZY AND IT MAKES YOU LAUGH. ACTING IN SLAPSTICK COMEDIES MUST BE REALLY HARD — LOOK HOW MANY ACCIDENTS ARE HAPPENING. BUT THE GREAT THING IS THAT NONE OF THE ACTORS EVER GET HURT, HOWEVER OFTEN THEY FALL FLAT ON THEIR FACES!

$10,000

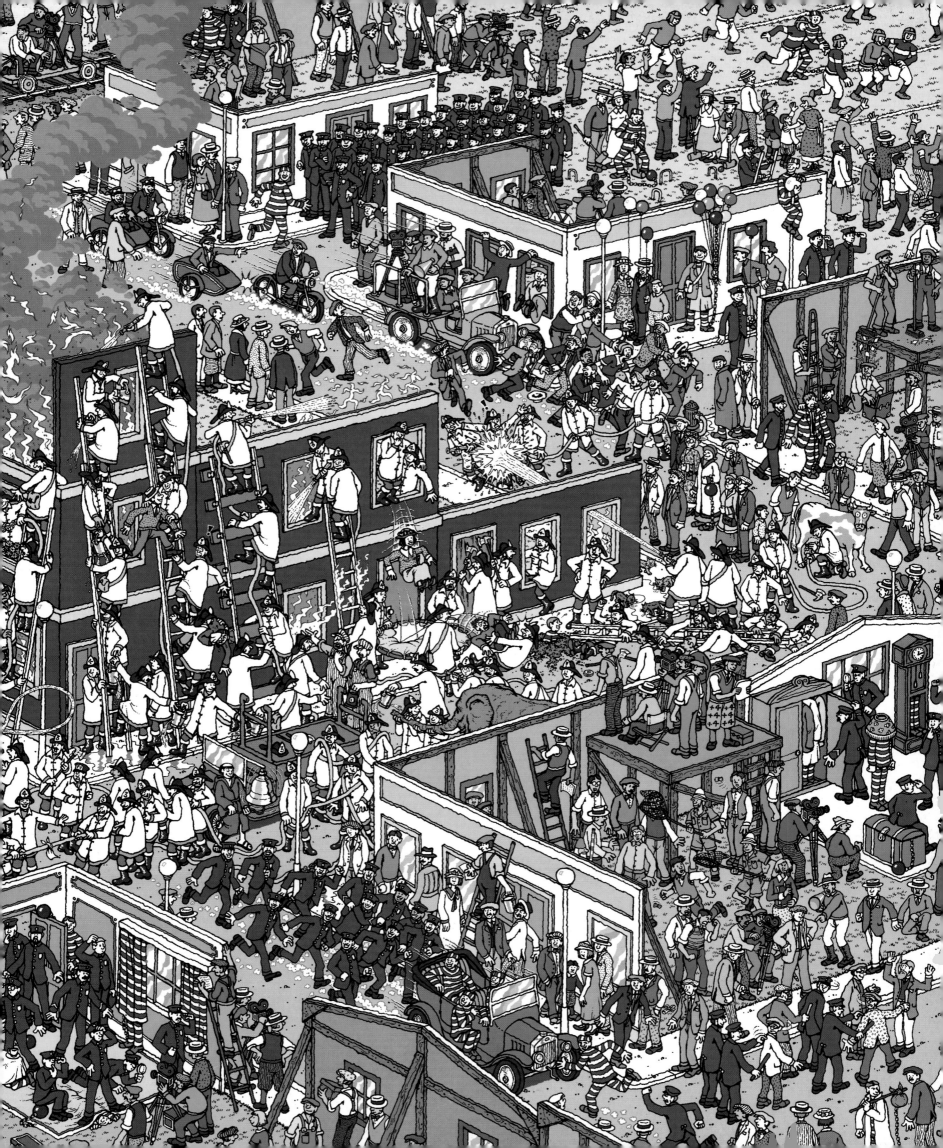

FUN IN THE FOREIGN LEGION

PHEW, MOVIE FANS, DON'T GET OVERHEATED. THIS IS THE MOST SIZZLING LOCATION SO FAR! EVERYONE'S SWELTERING, FROM STARS TO SAND-SHIFTERS. SOME OF THOSE EXTRAS LOOK LIKE THEY'RE LOSING THEIR COOL – HAVE THEY FORGOTTEN THIS IS ONLY A FILM? PERHAPS IT'S TIME A FEW MORE OF THEM DESERTED THE DESERT AND JOINED THE RUSH FOR ICE CREAM!

ALI BABA AND THE FORTY THIEVES

WHAT A CRUSH IN THE CAVE, WALDO-FOLLOWERS, BUT PAN IN ON THOSE POTS OF TREASURE! HOW MANY THIEVES WERE IN THE STORY? I BELIEVE THIS DIRECTOR THINKS FORTY THOUSAND! HAVE YOU SPOTTED ALI BABA? HE'S IN THE ALLEY, CUTTING HAIR – THE SCRIPTWRITER THINKS HIS NAME'S ALLEY BARBER! JANGLING GENIES – WHAT A FEARFULLY FUNNY FLICK THIS IS!

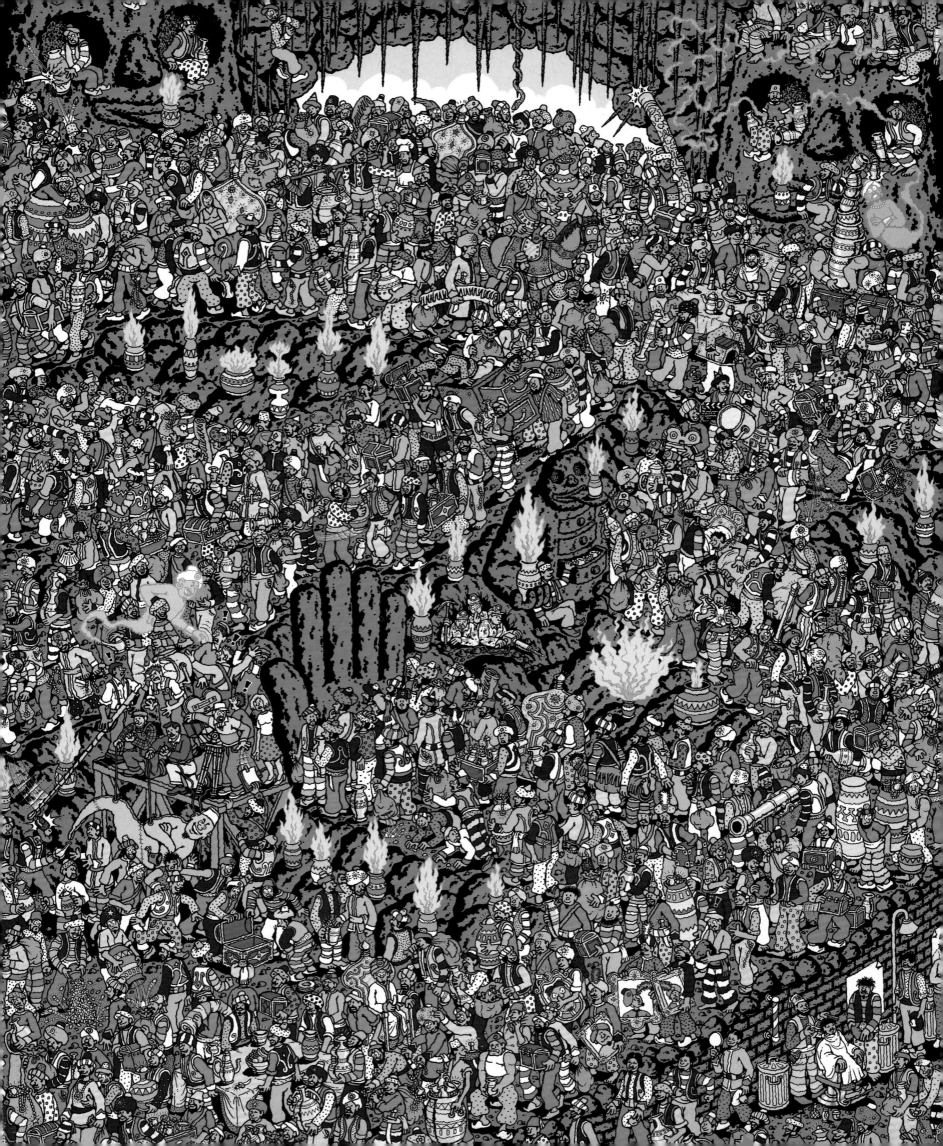

THE SWASHBUCKLING MUSKETEERS

ALL FOR ONE, ONE FOR ALL! — WASN'T THAT THE MOTTO OF THE THREE MUSKETEERS? NOW LOOK AT THIS FREE-FOR-ALL! CAN YOU SPOT OUR THREE GALLANT HEROES BATTLING WITH THE RED-COATED CARDINAL'S GUARDS? WITH ALL THIS SWASHBUCKLING ACTION GOING ON, I WONDER HOW THE CAMERAMEN CAN CAPTURE IT ALL ON FILM!

DINOSAURS, SPACEMEN, AND GHOULS

PHEW, INCREDIBLE! TIME, SPACE, AND HORROR ARE IN A MIGHTY MUDDLE HERE! WHAT COSMIC COSTUMES AND WHAT GREAT SPECIAL EFFECTS! ONE OF THOSE FLYING SAUCERS LOOKS LIKE IT'S REALLY FLYING! ARE THOSE REAL ALIENS INSIDE, NOT ACTORS AT ALL? SO WHAT'S REAL AND WHAT'S MADE UP IN FILMS LIKE THESE?

WHEN THE STARS COME OUT

WOW, WALDO-WATCHERS, THIS IS WHAT I CALL GLAMOUR! I'M AT A MAJOR MOVIE PREMIERE. THE STARS HAVE COME TO SEE THE FILM; THE CROWDS HAVE COME TO SEE THE STARS. LOOK AT THAT PINK STRETCH LIMO – NOW THAT'S A PERFECT CAR FOR A STAR. AND WHO'S IN THE BONE-MOBILE BEHIND? AND DOESN'T KING KONG LOOK NICER IN LIFE THAN WHEN HE'S ON THE SCREEN?

WHERE'S WALDO? THE MUSICAL

WOW, WHAT AN EXTRAVAGANZA, WALDO-WATCHERS — THIS ALL-SINGING, ALL-
DANCING MOVIE IS ALL ABOUT ME AND MY FRIENDS! LOOK HOW MANY ACTORS
ARE DRESSED UP AS ME! AND LOOK AT ALL THE WOOFS, WENDAS, WIZARD
WHITEBEARDS, AND ODLAWS. HAVE YOU NOTICED THAT THE WARDROBE
DEPARTMENT HAS MADE MISTAKES WITH SOME OF THE ACTORS' COSTUMES?
BUT THAT WON'T HELP YOU FIND THE REAL ME AND MY FOUR FRIENDS IN
THIS FILM! I'LL GIVE YOU SOME CLUES. I'M THE WALDO WITH SOMETHING EXTRA
FOR WOOF. ALL YOU CAN SEE OF THE REAL WOOF IS HIS TAIL. THE REAL
WENDA HAS A CAMERA. THE REAL WIZARD WHITEBEARD IS WEARING A HAT
BENT TO THE LEFT. AND THE REAL ODLAW IS HOLDING A WALKING STICK.
      THERE'S JUST ONE MORE THING. I'VE BEEN FOLLOWED HERE BY ONE
CHARACTER FROM EVERY SET I'VE VISITED. SO CAN YOU SPOT ALL ELEVEN OF
THEM IN THIS SCENE? AND CAN YOU FIND OUT WHEN EACH CHARACTER FIRST
JOINED ME, AND CATCH ALL THEIR APPEARANCES THROUGHOUT MY TRAVELS?

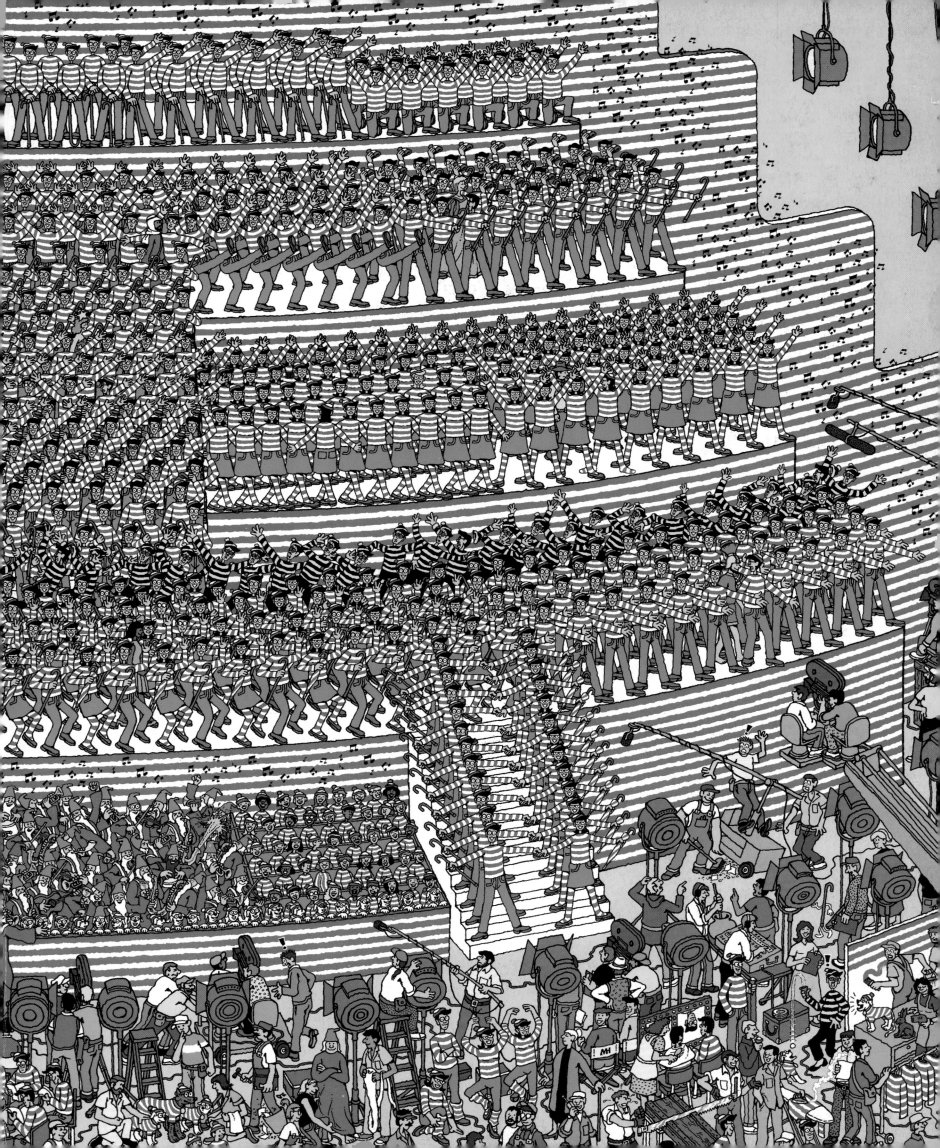

THE FABULOUS WHERE'S WALDO? IN HOLLYWOOD check list

Lots more things for Waldo-watchers to look for!

★ ★ ★ ★ ★ A DREAM COME TRUE ★ ★ ★ ★ ★

- A soldier capturing some food
- A double agent in a spy film
- Someone walking tall
- A swing band
- A green star on a yellow ball
- A wind machine blowing out of control
- A romantic scene
- A girl in a bathing suit with a yellow hat
- Eight pieces of heart-shaped film equipment
- Ten studio security guards
- Twenty-one pirates in striped clothing
- Three shields
- Someone who has put their foot in it
- Three people with skis
- A scenic painter
- A man with a red-and-white-spotted tie
- A friendly pirate

★ ★ ★ SHHH! THIS IS A SILENT MOVIE ★ ★ ★

- A watchtower
- Two mobile cameras
- A director with a giant megaphone
- A searchlight
- A runaway wheel
- Two butterfly catchers
- Thirteen balloons
- A man in plus four trousers
- Seven megaphones
- A trail of leaking buckets
- Nine four-legged animals
- Fifteen cameras
- Some flowers being watered
- Three men tripping on some fruit
- A hose cut by an ax
- Four fire chiefs wearing pointed hats
- A railway-track ladder
- Three men wearing red shirts and suspenders
- Two umbrellas

★ ★ ★ ★ ★ HORSEPLAY IN TROY ★ ★ ★ ★ ★

- Five blue soldiers with red-crested helmets
- One soldier wearing sandals
- Thirteen real four-legged animals
- Some ancient traffic police
- Five red soldiers with blue-crested helmets
- Two soldiers with slings
- Four first aid soldiers
- Five yellow soldiers with blue-crested helmets
- Five soldiers with brooms
- One soldier with a square shield
- Three movie crew members wearing sunglasses
- Three soldiers with extra-long cloaks
- Two statues waving at each other
- Three Trojans drinking coffee
- Ten arrows that are stuck in shields
- A trash can
- Soldiers arguing about the time

★ ★ ★ FUN IN THE FOREIGN LEGION ★ ★ ★

- Some date trees
- Twelve camels
- A modern airplane ruining a camera shot
- Four trees surrendering
- A rock hitting sixteen people
- Two men being shaken out of a tree
- The right costumes in the wrong colors
- A horseman riding in the wrong direction
- A French flag with colors in the wrong order
- Five men wearing undershirts and boxers
- Some enemies fighting back to back
- An unpopular musician
- A man reading a newspaper
- Three men hiding underneath animals
- An animal stepping on a man's foot
- A man surrendering to a shovel

★ ★ A TREMENDOUS SONG AND DANCE ★ ★

- One dancer wearing a blue carnation
- Some tap dancers
- A grand piano
- A musician playing a double bass
- Dancers wearing top hats and tails
- Sailors saluting the ship's "N" sign
- The captain's log
- Sailors with bell-bottom pants
- A vice admiral
- A piano keyboard
- Four orange feathers
- A soldier on the wrong set
- Five real anchors
- Three watery creatures
- Nine mops
- Four sailors with tattoos

★ ★ ALI BABA AND THE FORTY THIEVES ★ ★

- A man asleep in bed
- Another man awake in bed
- Five animals
- A man wearing yellow shoes
- A man wearing green shoes
- A man wearing a red shoe and a white shoe
- A man wearing a red shoe and a pink shoe
- A chest of drawers
- A man with jewels in his beard
- Two careless carpet carriers
- A man wearing a green turban
- A man wearing a yellow turban
- Four real genies
- A man carrying a gray treasure chest
- A man with a red star on his turban
- A man with a yellow tassel on his fez
- A man with a green tassel on his fez

★ ★ ★ ★ THE WILD, WILD WEST ★ ★ ★ ★ ★

- Two cowboys about to draw against each other
- Drinkers raising their glasses to a lady
- Outlaws holding up a stagecoach
- Some boisterous cowboys painting the town red
- Doc holiday
- The film wardrobe department
- Buffalo Bill
- The loan ranger
- Gamblers playing cards
- A couple of gunslingers
- Calamity Jane
- A buffalo **stamp**ede
- A spaghetti western
- A horse drawn wagon
- Billy the kid
- Townspeople saluting General Store
- A band of outlaws
- Two cowboys shouting, "This town ain't big enough for the both of us."

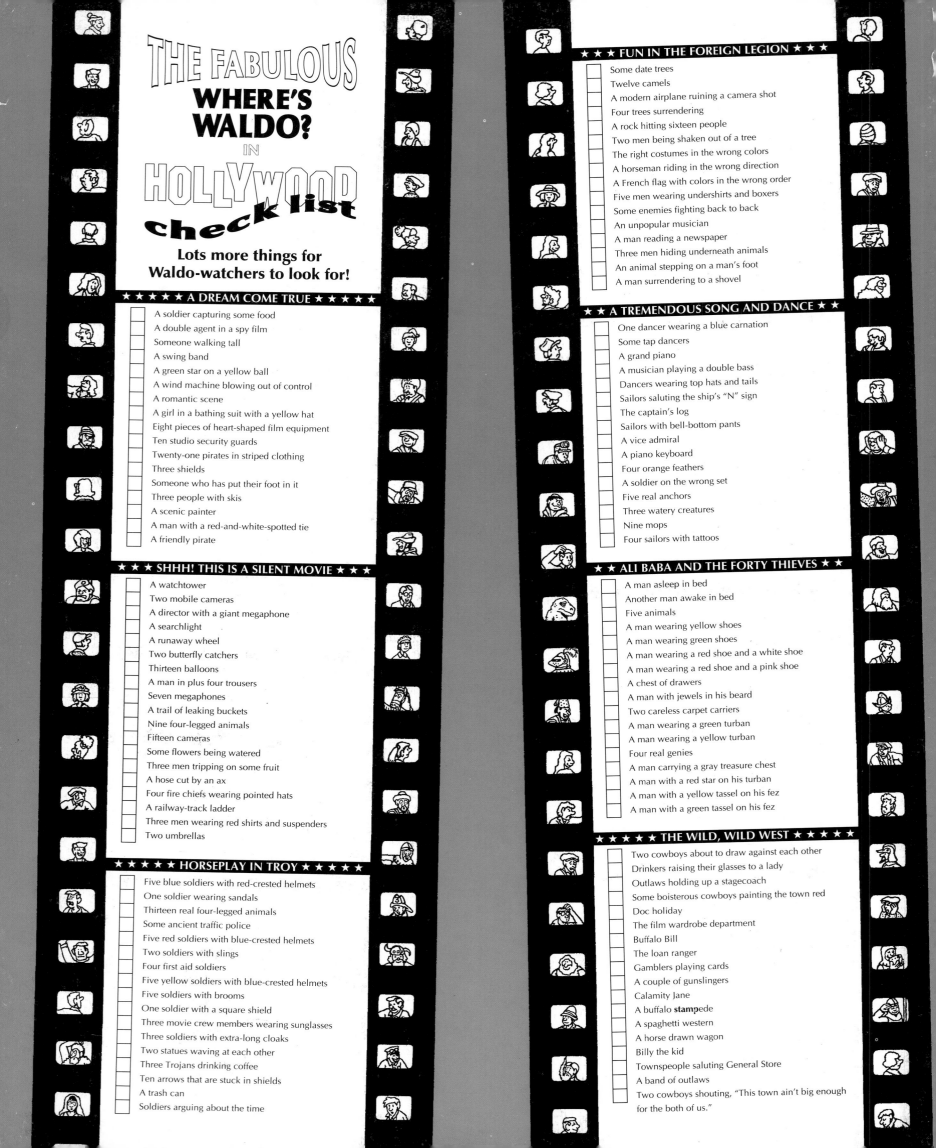